Flora the Fairy

Tony Bradman ★ Emma Carlow

Green Bananas

Crabtree Publishing Company
www.crabtreebooks.com

PMB 16A, 350 Fifth Avenue,
Suite 3308,
New York, NY 10118

616 Welland Avenue,
St. Catharines, Ontario
Canada, L2M 5V6

Bradman, Tony.
  Flora the fairy / Tony Bradman ; illustrated by Emma Carlow.
  p. cm. -- (Green bananas)
  Summary: Some fairy magic helps Flora overcome her fear of Rufus the cat
when she goes to visit her Grandma and Grandpa.   .
  ISBN-13: 978-0-7787-1022-6 (rlb) -- ISBN-10: 0-7787-1022-X (rlb)
  ISBN-13: 978-0-7787-1038-7 (pbk) -- ISBN-10: 0-7787-1038-6 (pbk)
  [1. Cats--Fiction. 2. Fear--Fiction. 3. Fairies--Fiction. 4.
Grandparents--Fiction.] I. Carlow, Emma, ill. II. Title. III. Series.
  PZ7.B7275Fl 2005 [E]--dc22

2005001571 LC

Published by Crabtree Publishing in 2005
First published in 2005 by Egmont Books Ltd.
Text copyright © Tony Bradman 2005
Illustrations copyright © Emma Carlow 2005
The author and illustrator have asserted their moral rights.
Paperback ISBN 0-7787-1038-6
Reinforced Hardcover Binding ISBN 0-7787-1022-X

Cat Trouble

 Feeling Bad

Making
Friends

For Lily and Oscar . . .

and Rufus, of course!

T.B.

To my neighbours,

Flora and Rufus

E.C.

Cat Trouble

Mom was taking Flora the Fairy to Grandma's and Grandpa's house. Flora didn't want to go.

I'll be late!

Grandma and Grandpa were going
to look after her while Mom
went shopping.

Here
we are!

Flora loved them . . . but they had

a cat named Rufus.

And Flora was scared of him.

Flora didn't like the way Rufus

walked softly and silently.

She didn't like the way he followed

her around.

And she didn't like the way he
stared at her with his big scary
green eyes.

Mom knocked on the door, and
Grandma opened it.

See you later!

Rufus didn't seem to be around, so Flora went in. Mom kissed her and flew off.

Grandma took Flora into the
kitchen.

She sat at the table and began to draw.

Behind her the cat flap opened slowly . . .

Creeeak!

welcome

Flora turned around – and there was Rufus, creeping up on her! He was staring at her with his big scary green eyes.

Flora screamed.

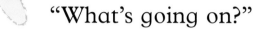

"What's going on?"

said Grandpa. They tried

to calm Flora down.

But it was no use.

Feeling Bad

"Please put Rufus outside again!"
Flora said. So Grandpa did what
she asked – and locked the cat flap.

Flora calmed down at last. She helped Grandma do some mixing and stirring. But Flora could see Rufus through the window.

She thought he looked sad.

Miaow!

Next, Grandpa read Flora her
favorite story. But Rufus was outside
Grandpa's window . . .

Flora thought he sounded lonely.

Then they had a drink and

something to eat, and watched T.V.

But Rufus was outside that window

as well . . .

Flora thought he might be hungry too.

Oh no, it's raining!

Now Flora felt bad. Rufus was outside because of her!

It's all my fault!

Grandma and Grandpa didn't look

very happy either.

Poor Rufus!

"I think he's trying to tell you something, Flora," said Grandpa. "Shall we let him in and find out what it is?" said Grandma.

But Flora was still scared of Rufus.

"I've got an idea!" said Grandpa suddenly. He whispered in Grandma's ear, and Grandma smiled.

Making Friends

"How would you like to play a special game, Flora?" said Grandma. "Now, where did I put those old face paints?"

Flora sat very still while Grandma painted her face.

Soon Flora looked exactly like . . .

a cat!

Terrific!

Grandma and Grandpa waved their wands . . . and Flora could feel herself changing.

AlakaZOO!
AlakaZAM!

She was a cat!

She walked softly and silently. She stared at Grandma and Grandpa with her big eyes.

Nice pussy cat!

Purrrr!

She was following them, and
rubbing against their legs!

So now she knew. Rufus walked

quietly because that's what cats do.

And he stared at her and followed her around because he liked her!

Grandma and Grandpa waved their wands . . . and Flora was herself again.

She went straight to the cat flap and

let Rufus in.

Flora looked into his big green eyes.

They weren't so scary any more.

I want
to stay!

And later, when Mom came to

take Flora home . . .

Guess who didn't want to go!

Flora and Rufus touched noses and made friends.

Purrr!